On Rosh Hashanah
and Yom Kippur

On Rosh Hashanah and Yom Kippur

La Shana Tova

BY CATHY GOLDBERG FISHMAN

ILLUSTRATED BY MELANIE W. HALL

ALADDIN PAPERBACKS
NEW YORK LONDON TORONTO SYDNEY SINGAPORE

Other books in this series:

On Passover
On Purim
On Hanukkah

First Aladdin Paperbacks edition September 2000

Aladdin Paperbacks
An imprint of Simon & Schuster
Children's Publishing Division
1230 Avenue of the Americas
New York, NY 10020

Also available in an Atheneum Books for Young Readers hardcover edition

Jacket design by Nina Barnett
The text for this book was set in Novarese.
The illustrations were rendered in collagraph and mixed media.

Printed in Hong Kong

10 9 8 7 6 5 4 3 2 1

The Library of Congress has cataloged the hardcover
edition as follows:

Fishman, Cathy.
On Rosh Hashanah and Yom Kippur / by Cathy Goldberg Fishman; illustrated by Melanie W. Hall.
p. cm.
Summary: As she and her family celebrate these two Jewish holidays, a young girl contemplates their meaning in her life.
ISBN 0-689-80526-8 (hc.)
1. Rosh ha-Shanah—Juvenile literature. 2. Yom Kippur—Juvenile literature. [1. Rosh ha-Shanah.
2. Yom Kippur. 3. High Holidays. 4. Fasts and feasts—Judaism.] I. Hall, Melanie W., ill. II. Title.
BM695.N5F57   1997
296.4'31—dc20
96-23258

ISBN 0-689-83892-1 (Aladdin pbk.)

To Hannah Gillman Fishman yl"a
and Sidney Fishman zt"l
for the warmth of their holiday table
—C. G. F.

For Megan, a true-blue friend
—M. W. H.

$\mathcal{I}$ can tell when it is time for Rosh Hashanah and Yom Kippur. I don't even have to look on the calendar.

I can tell because we get a lot of mail. Every year people we know send cards to wish me and my family a happy and healthy new year. *La Shana Tova*, they say in Hebrew.

I see the leaves change from shades of green to browns and reds and yellows. I even feel the air change from warm and stuffy to cool and crisp. This is near the time of year when the seasons change from summer to fall. This is the time for the High Holy Days, Rosh Hashanah and Yom Kippur.

My sisters show me the place for Rosh Hashanah, the Jewish New Year, on my Jewish calendar. It is the first two days of the Hebrew month of Tishri.

"Why do we celebrate the new year in the seventh month?" I ask.

"Because," my sisters answer, "the Torah tells us to. The seventh month is special, just like the seventh day of the week, Shabbat, is special."

"Rosh Hashanah is not the new year in terms of months," my mother says. "It is the new year for how we think and act."

Grandmother nods. "It is also the day when God created the world."

"That means that Rosh Hashanah is the world's birthday!" says my brother.

On Rosh Hashanah eve, I help my mother bless and light the holiday candles before we eat the New Year's meal. I watch the candles glow as we thank God for bringing us all together. We pray for a new year of joy and good health and peace.

May the holiday candles shine brightly for the New Year

I see round apples and round raisin-filled *challah*, the special bread we eat on Rosh Hashanah. They are round like the cycle of the year is round.

My sisters say the blessing over the challah. I
get to say the blessing over the apples. We dip
the apples and challah in honey and pray that this
new year will be sweet—as sweet as honey and
apples and challah taste.

May your New Year be a sweet one

We go to *synagogue* on Rosh Hashanah day. We wear new clothes to help us celebrate a new year. I see my rabbi dressed in a white robe. I see the Torah in its white holiday cover.

"Why are they in white?" my brother asks.

"Because," I whisper back, "it is the color of forgiveness."

Then the rabbi chants from the Torah. He chants the story of Abraham and Isaac.

In synagogue we pray and listen to the *shofar*,
the curved horn of a ram. I stand on tiptoe and
crane my neck so I can see the Ba'al Tekiyah blow
the shofar.

"*Tekiyah, shevarim, teruah,*" the rabbi softly calls
out the notes for the Ba'al Tekiyah to play.

The shofar gives one long, loud blast, then
three medium, wailing blasts, and finally, I hear
nine short blasts that sound as if someone is
sobbing.

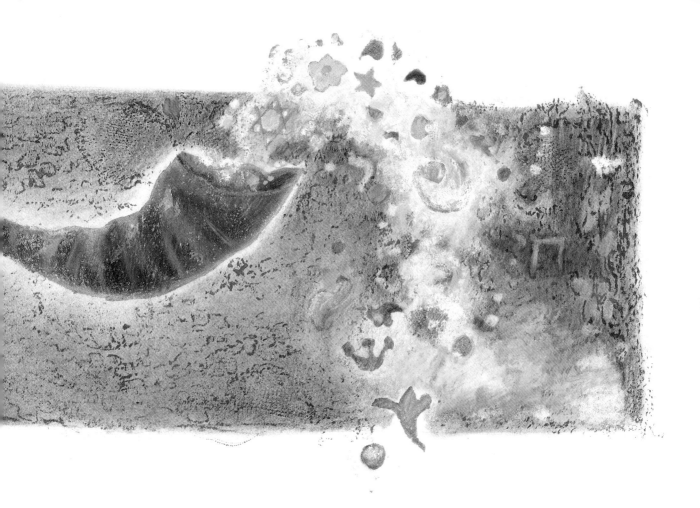

The sound of the shofar reminds me of God. It makes me think about everything I need to do to be a better person.

May the sound of the Shofar bring a year that's full of joy, love, and good cheer

We pray and call God our Father, our King. We pray and call God our Judge. The rabbi says that Rosh Hashanah is when God inscribes our names in the Book of Life for the coming year. I imagine that he writes down everything about me in that book. I want what he writes to be good.

In the afternoon, I go with my family to the river. While Grandfather chants the *Tashlich* prayers, I search deep in my pockets for tiny bits of crumbs or lint. I pretend that the bits of lint are all of my bad deeds and thoughts of the past year and I throw them into the water. As they float away, I promise to try to do better during the new year.

When Rosh Hashanah is over we wait for Yom Kippur, the Day of Atonement, to start. As we wait, we try to feel closer to God. I think about the good things that he wants me to do. I put part of my allowance in my special *tzedakah* box. I give the box to my rabbi so he can help people who are in need.

The tenth day of Tishri is Yom Kippur. It is a day of fasting and I skip all my snacks. Mother and Father do not eat anything at all. I see books on our dining table instead of food.

"We eat nothing at all from sundown to sundown," my father says. "On Yom Kippur we feed our minds and our souls, not our bodies."

On Yom Kippur we go back to synagogue and pray some more. We try to atone for the times when we did not do our best. We say we are sorry for any bad thing we have done. . . .

I say I am sorry to my friends; I say I am sorry to my family; I say I am sorry to God.

We all forgive and ask to be forgiven.

The rabbi chants from the Book of Jonah. We listen and then pray some more.

At the end of the service, after sunset, the shofar is blown again.

"*Tekiyah gedolah*," the rabbi calls softly.

The Ba'al Tekiyah makes the shofar blast as long and as loudly as he can.

We feel clean and good inside. I feel proud—ready to start a good new year and be the best that I can be.

Then we gather with friends and break the fast
with another holiday meal.

All of us
wish you
the best for
a Happy
New
Year

Every year we get a lot of cards. I line them up on a table where everyone can see. But I remember something special that I didn't see on any of the cards that came in the mail. So I make my own card and put it on the table, too.

 # GLOSSARY

Ba'al Tekiyah (BAH all teh kee YAH): the person who blows the shofar.

Challah (KHAL lah): a specially braided egg bread used for Jewish holiday meals.

La Shana Tova (lah shah NAH toe VAH): Hebrew for "a good year."

Shabbat (shah BHAT): Hebrew for Sabbath, the seventh day of the week, which is Saturday. A day of rest and worship in the Jewish religion.

Shevarim (sheh vah REEM): three broken notes played on the shofar.

Shofar (show FAR): a hollow ram's horn that is blown during the month before Tishri, on Rosh Hashanah, and at the end of Yom Kippur.

Synagogue (SIN a gog): the central house of worship for the Jewish community, sometimes called a temple.

Tashlich (TASH leekh): a religious ceremony held near a flowing body of water symbolizing the casting away of sins.

Tekiyah (teh KEE yah): one long, loud note played on the shofar.

Tekiyah Gedolah (teh KEE yah gah DOE lah): one prolonged, loud blast played on the shofar.

Teruah (teh ROO ah): nine short, choppy notes played on the shofar.

 Tishri (TISH ree): the seventh month of the ancient Hebrew calendar, which corresponds to September/October.

Torah (tor RAH): the Five Books of Moses.

Tzedakah (tseh DUH kah): money or other help given as a religious obligation to help the needy.